The Fairies of Pixie Hollow

Adapted by Natasha Bouchard

Illustrated by the Disney Storybook Artists

A GOLDEN BOOK • NEW YORK

ISBN: 978-0-375-87493-2

www.randomhouse.com/kids/disney

MANUFACTURED IN MALAYSIA

10 9 8 7 6 5 4 3 2 1

The Never fairies live in the enchanted world of Pixie Hollow, where magic happens every day.

Queen Clarion is the kind ruler of the Never fairies.

Every Never fairy has a special talent. Tinker Bell is the best pots-and-pans-talent fairy in Pixie Hollow.

Tink is always ready to lend a helping hand . . . or a hammer!

The toughest repairs are Tink's favorites.
Help her put this object back together by connecting the dots.

Tink's room is filled with all her favorite things,
including her fuzzy pom-pom slippers.
How many different pairs can you find?

ANSWER:

Tink's friend Bess is Pixie Hollow's most talented artist.

Bess's studio is a mess!
Help Bess find her special double-sided paintbrush.

ANSWER:

Bess has drawn a picture of Tink.

Are you an artist like Bess?
Draw a picture of your favorite fairy here!

Lily is a garden-talent fairy. She loves plants, and they love her.

Lily's garden is overflowing with beautiful blossoms!
Help fill in the rest of the flowers.

Lily's friend Rosetta is also a garden-talent fairy. Rosetta spends almost as much time on her hair as she does on her garden!

Rosetta always plans her outfits in advance.
Help her match her tops and bottoms!

ANSWER: A-4; B-3; C-1; D-2.

Fira, a light-talent fairy, loves the sun, but she also loves the moon and stars. Help Fira connect the dots to find a constellation! Can you guess what it's called?

ANSWER: The Mermaid.

When Fira isn't napping or working,
she likes to read in the Home Tree library.

Fira loves anything that sparkles and shines.
Her room is full of things that are as bright as the sun.

Fira is the brightest of the light-talent fairies.
She even trains fireflies to light up Pixie Hollow at night.

Fira's friend Iridessa is a light-talent fairy, too.

Which picture of Iridessa is different? Circle it.

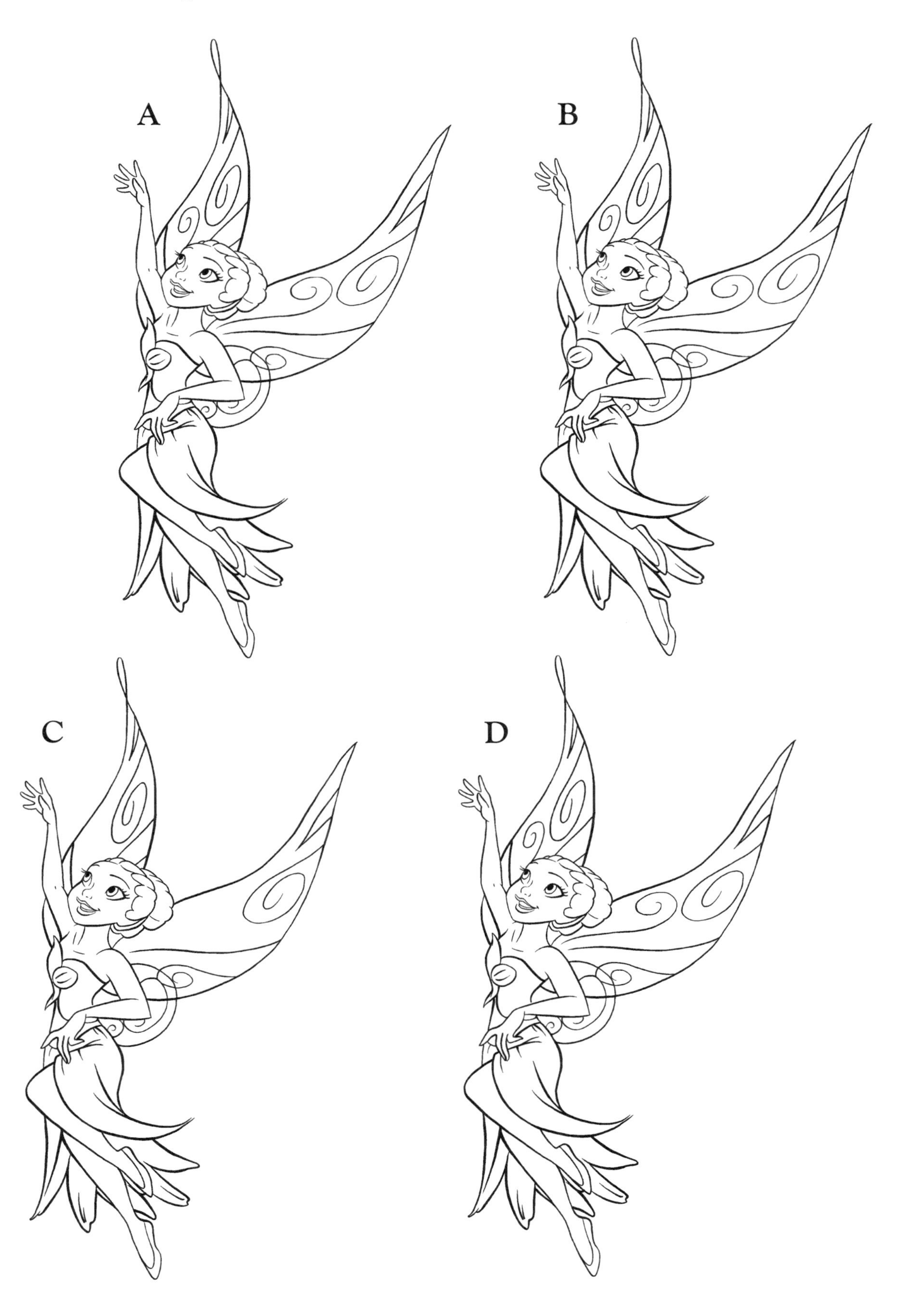

ANSWER: C.

Like all light-talent fairies, Iridessa loves glittering jewels.
Help Iridessa find her favorite gem!

Circle the jewel that matches this one:

Vidia is the fastest-flying fairy in Pixie Hollow.
She's also the meanest.

Circle the picture of Vidia that is different.

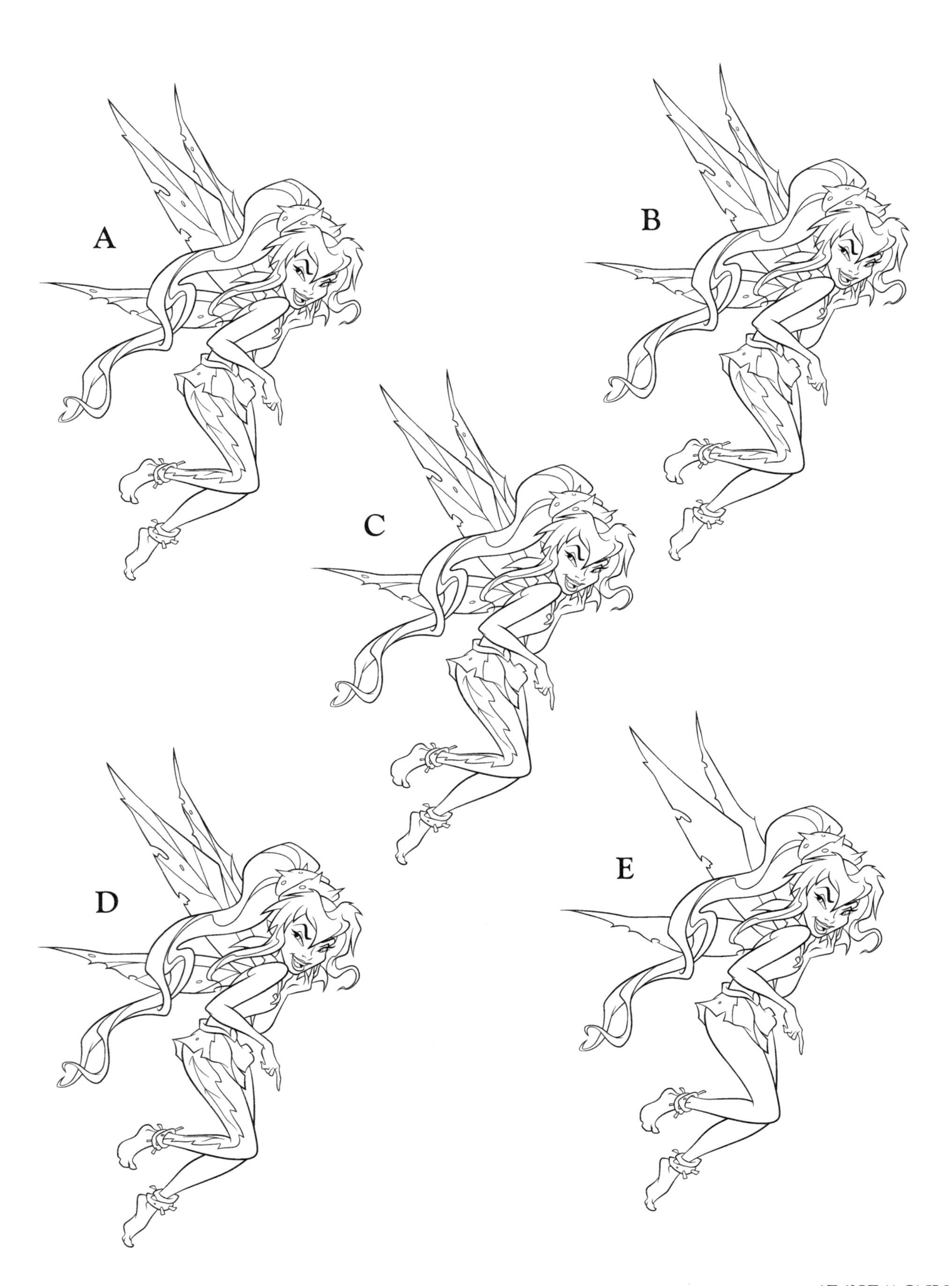

ANSWER: E.

The Never fairies love to play fairy tag!

Tink is trying to tag her friend Prilla in this game of fairy tag.
Follow each of the lines to see which one leads to Prilla.

ANSWER: A.

Prilla is one of the newest fairies in Pixie Hollow.

Help Prilla decorate her room.

Vidia
Tink
Beck
Lily
Rani
Fira
Prilla
Bess
Vidia
Tink
Beck
Lily
Rani
Fira
Prilla
Bess
Vidia
Tink
Beck
Lily
Rani
Fira
Prilla
Bess

When Prilla arrived in Pixie Hollow,
she didn't know what her talent was.

But Prilla soon learned that she has a talent all her own.
In the blink of an eye, she can travel to the mainland
and help children to believe in fairies.

What do fairies call humans?

Fairy manners are different than Clumsy manners. When Clumsies would say "Pleased to meet you," what would fairies say instead?

One of Prilla's best friends is a water-talent fairy, Rani.
Rani can do almost anything with water.
She can even form it into different shapes!

As a water-talent fairy, Rani loves boating on the rivers and streams of Pixie Hollow. Help Rani find her way through Havendish Stream to the swimming hole.

A magical bird named Mother Dove watches over all of Pixie Hollow. The special egg in her nest protects the magic of Never Land.

Rani and Tink would like some tasty fairy treats to go with their tea. Draw some food on the table for them.

Fairies love a good meal!

Silvermist is also a water-talent fairy.

Silvermist has received a message from Tink.
It says "Meet me at Havendish Stream!"

Tink flies around, waiting for Silvermist.

Terence helps make sure every fairy receives her daily share of fairy dust. He belongs to the fairy-dust talent.

Beck, an animal-talent fairy, can often be found in the forest visiting with her animal friends.

Beck can speak with any animal.

Beck loves taking care of her animal friends.

Beck hears a chipmunk pal calling for her.

Like her animal friends, Fawn is a bundle of energy, and she's always ready to play!

Fawn loves all animals.

Fairies love butterfly races. Whose butterfly will win the race? Trace the lines to find out whether Fawn's or Beck's is the winner.

Beck was very shy when she first arrived in Pixie Hollow. She spent almost all her time with her woodland friends. But these days she is also making many fairy friends.

Beck has found a tunnel! Take Beck to the end of this burrow to meet her rabbit friend.

You can see why Beck loves visiting the forest so much!

A fairy has lost her way in the woods. Help her get through the forest and back to the safety of Pixie Hollow. Be careful to avoid the dangerous hawk!

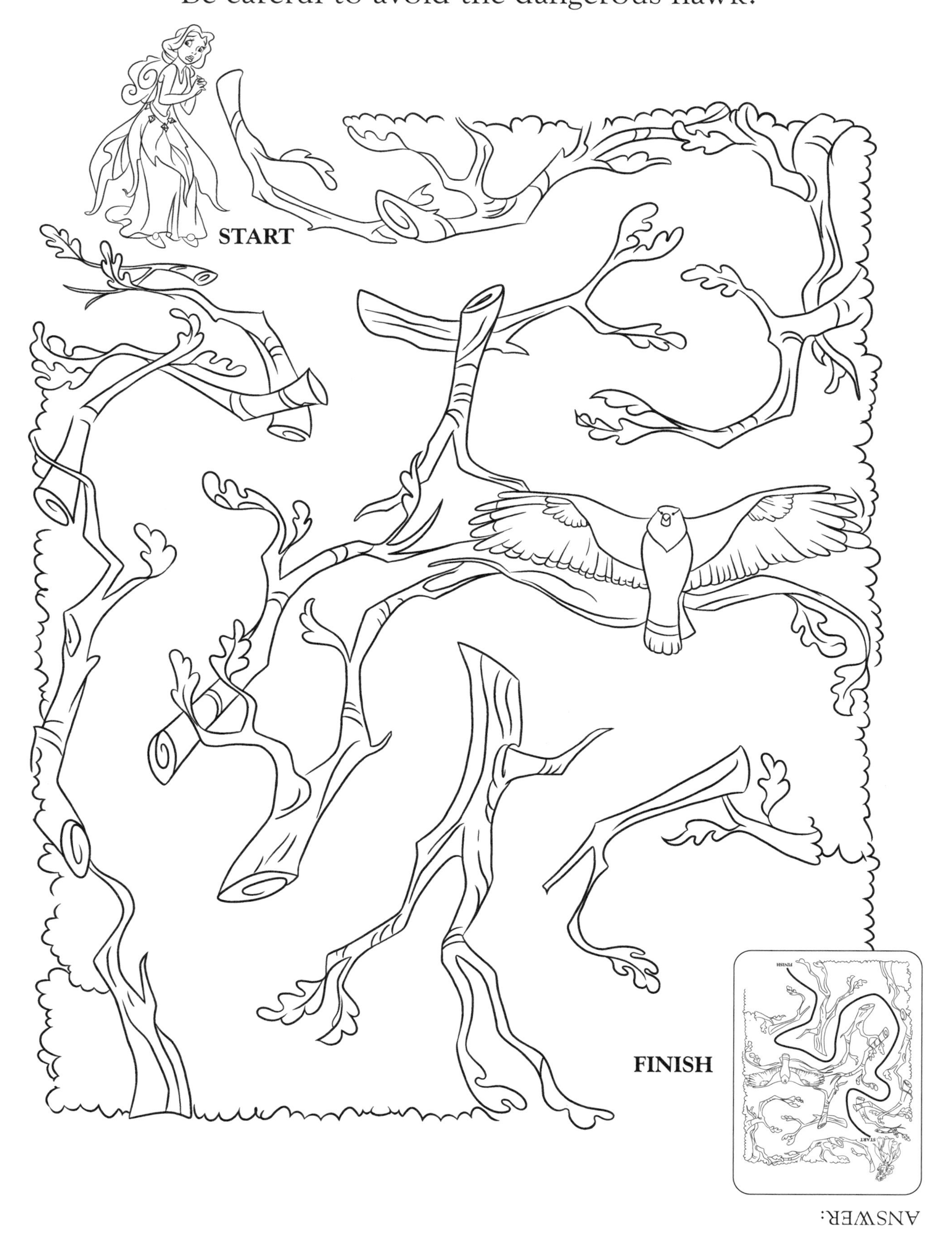

This fairy has just arrived in Pixie Hollow, and she isn't sure what her talent is! Help her figure it out, and give her an outfit and some tools that match her talent!

The Fairy Dance is coming up soon!
Even Mother Dove is excited!

The kitchen is very busy. Everyone is making delicious fairy foods for the dance, such as sugarplum tea cakes.

Dulcie, a baking-talent fairy, makes many treats,
but her specialty is poppy puff rolls!
Draw some more yummy food.

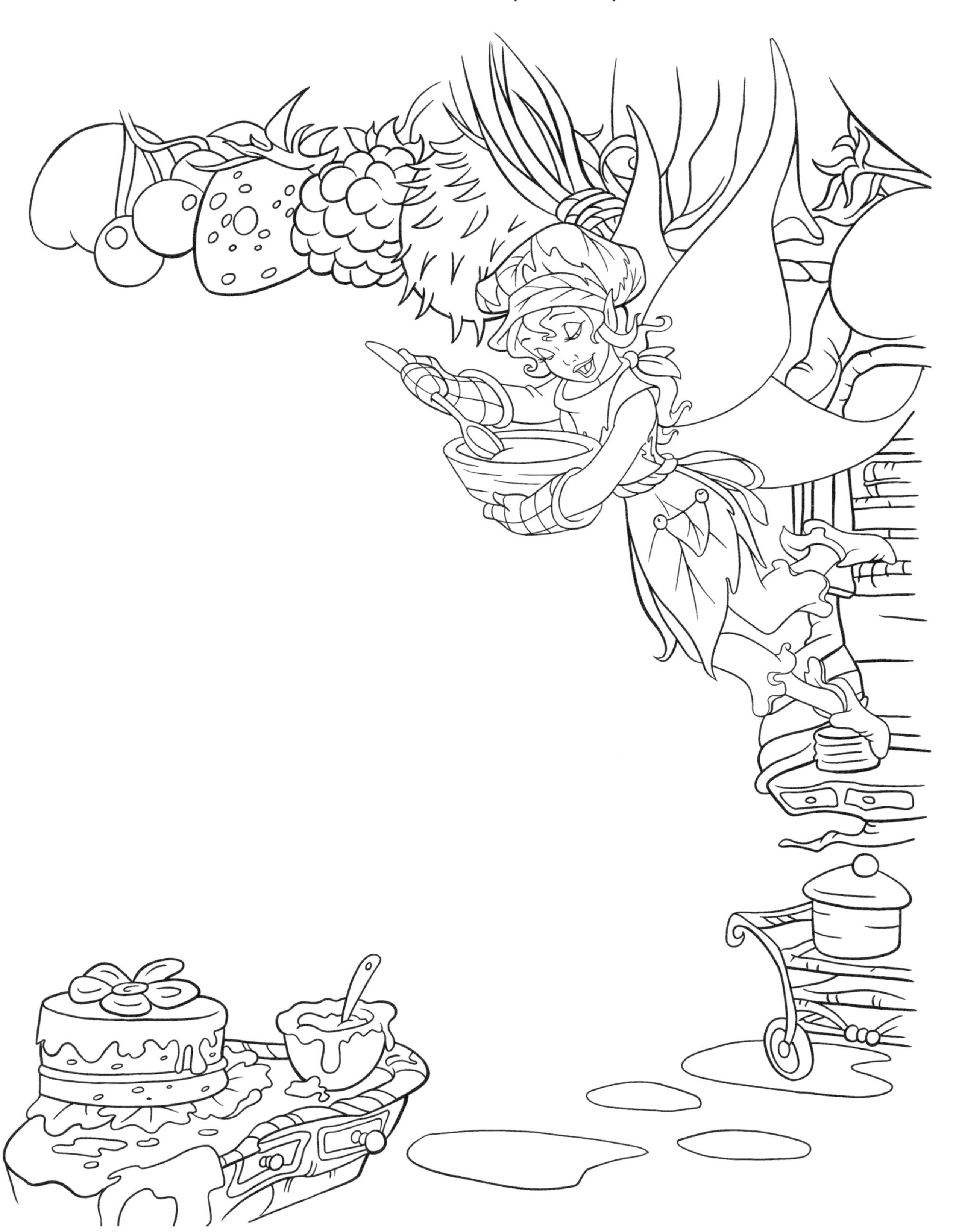

Prilla is getting dressed for the dance,
but she can't find anything fancy enough to wear!

Help Prilla make this plain dress fancy.

Extra care goes into Queen Clarion's special gown for the dance. This dress is made almost entirely out of rose petals!

Every fairy loves wearing a fancy dress.

Draw a dress for your favorite fairy. What details do you want to add? Maybe spider silk and plum leaves?

Take Fira to the fairy circle. She has to get ready to put on her special light show at the dance.

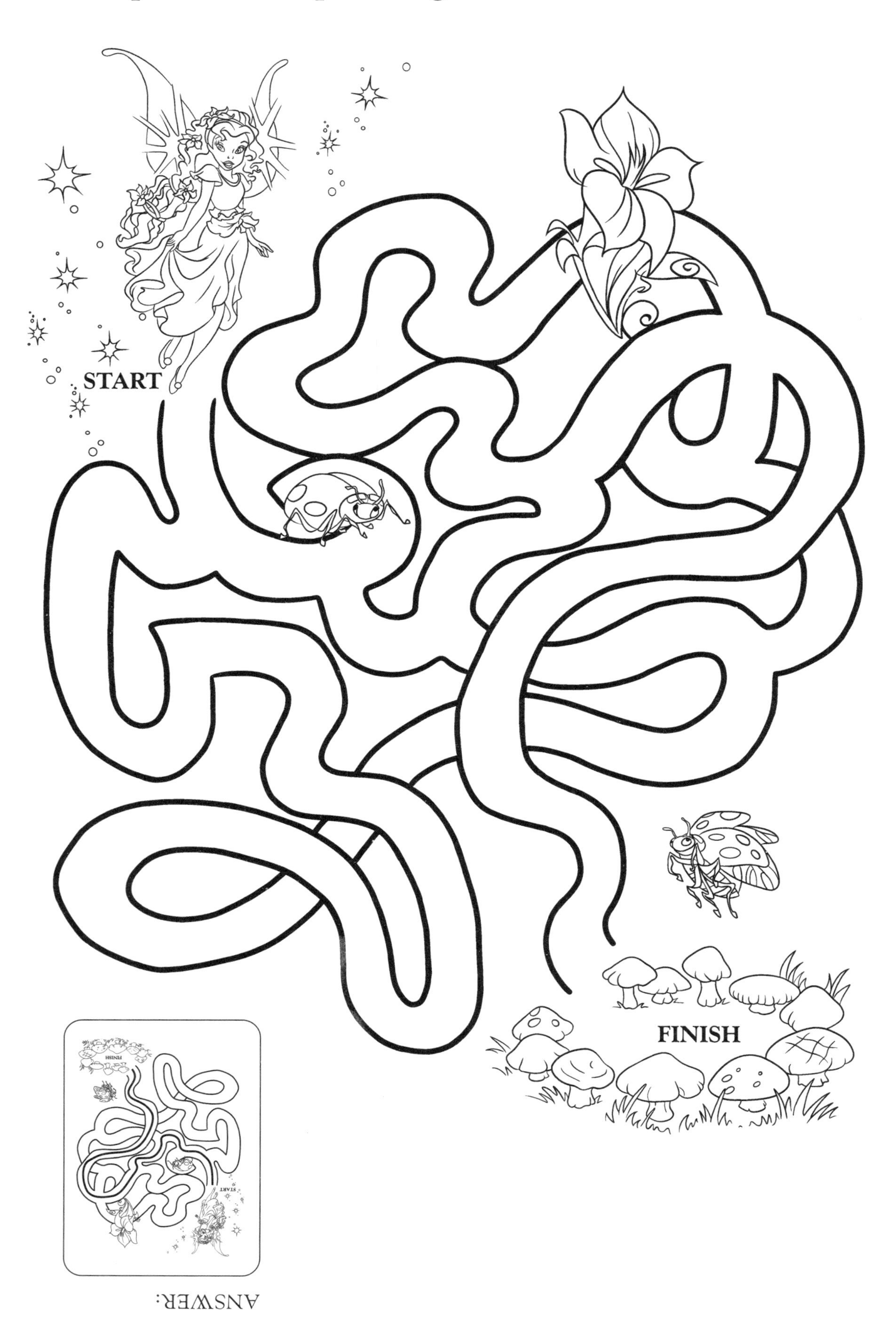

Music-talent fairies practice for the dance.

The Never fairies all have a wonderful time working together to make the dance special!